Donkey Ollie's

# CHRISTMAS in HEAVEN

By Brian Stewart

Adapted and Directed by Doug Aberle

CG Artwork supervised by Alexander Aberle

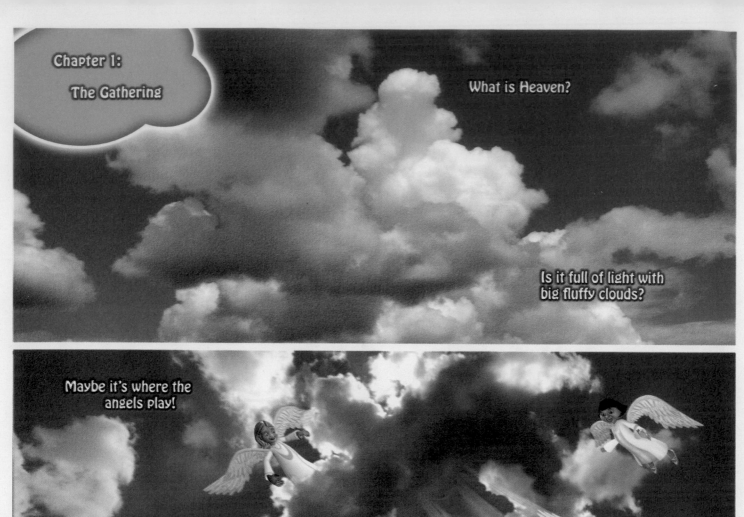

It is a place of fun...

... and delight...

... and beauty!

And it is a place where everyone gets along!

Everyone, that is, except Donkey Ollie's brothers!

"Come on, Esau!" exclaimed Ollie, "Play fair!"

"I never felt my tail being tagged!" complained Esau.

"I did so touch your tail!" Isa responded.

"If your tail is tagged, you're it!"

"I saw the whole thing!" added Jeremy. "What happened?"

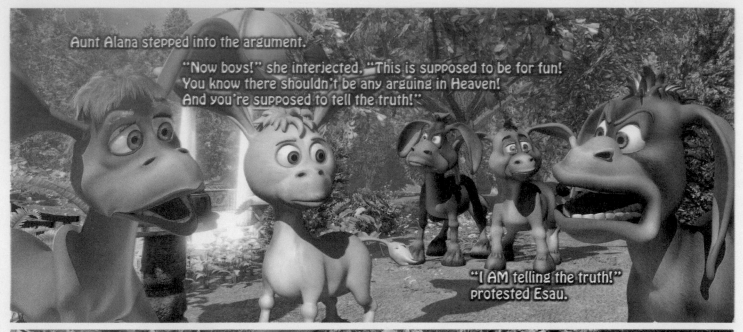

Aunt Alana stepped into the argument.

"Now boys!" she interjected. "This is supposed to be for fun! You know there shouldn't be any arguing in Heaven! And you're supposed to tell the truth!"

"I AM telling the truth!" protested Esau.

"I never felt Isa touch my tail! Besides," Esau continued, "I'm much quicker than he is. It would be impossible for him to ever touch my tail!"

"Okay," said Ollie. "Then let's settle this with a race!"

"A race? asked Esau.

"If you beat him, Esau," said Ollie, "then we will take your word for it... he didn't touch your tail. If Isa wins, you have to give all the kids donkey rides!"

"I'll race him," said Isa. "I'll beat him, too!"

"Where would they race to?" asked Jeremy.

"GO!" Ollie yelled.   Both donkeys took off and raced down the path as fast as they could!

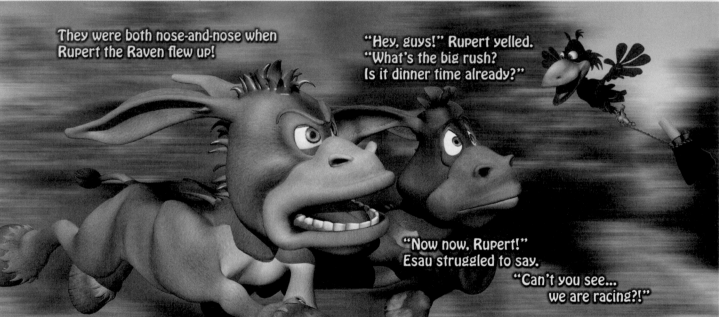

They were both nose-and-nose when Rupert the Raven flew up!

"Hey, guys!" Rupert yelled. "What's the big rush? Is it dinner time already?"

"Now now, Rupert!" Esau struggled to say.

"Can't you see... we are racing?!"

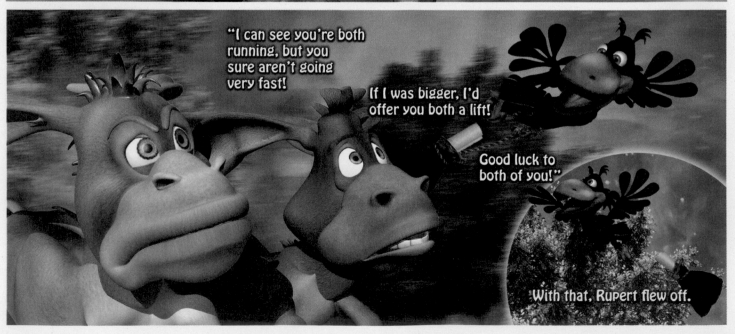

"I can see you're both running, but you sure aren't going very fast!

If I was bigger, I'd offer you both a lift!

Good luck to both of you!"

With that, Rupert flew off.

Both donkeys pushed on, as fast as they could go. They both made it to the half-way point...

... circled around the fountain...

... and then headed back!!

They were both getting a bit out of breath. Esau was slightly in the lead!

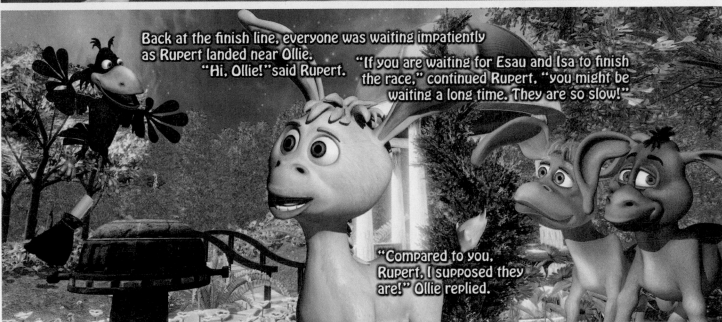

Back at the finish line, everyone was waiting impatiently as Rupert landed near Ollie.
"Hi, Ollie!" said Rupert.

"If you are waiting for Esau and Isa to finish the race," continued Rupert, "you might be waiting a long time. They are so slow!"

"Compared to you, Rupert, I supposed they are!" Ollie replied.

The sheep landed near the edge of the Crystal Creek, just as the dolphins popped up, singing.

"Greetings, greetings, greetings from the sea! Praise and honor and glory to the king!"

"Greetings, greetings our brothers on the shore!"

"We come to hear the news!"

"Tell us, tell us more!"

A great many animals came to the farm from all over Heaven. Horses, monkeys, camels, bears... they all came to hear Rupert.

"I think that's everyone. Ollie!" said Rupert.

"Besides, I'm tired of waiting! I've just got to share the news with everyone!"

Rupert began to sing.

"Listen up, my friends! This will affect you all!"

"Everyone is invited to partake in a play about the Savior!"

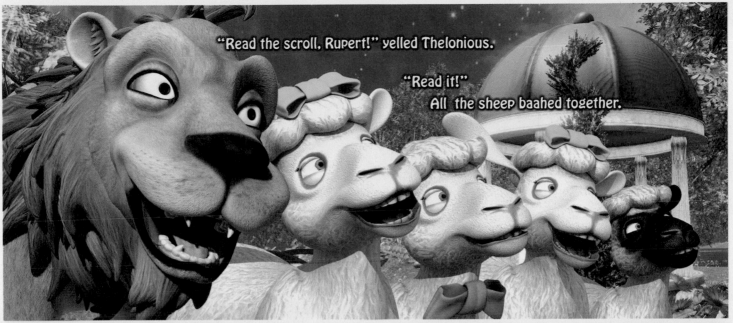

"Read the scroll, Rupert!" yelled Thelonious.

"Read it!"
All the sheep baahed together.

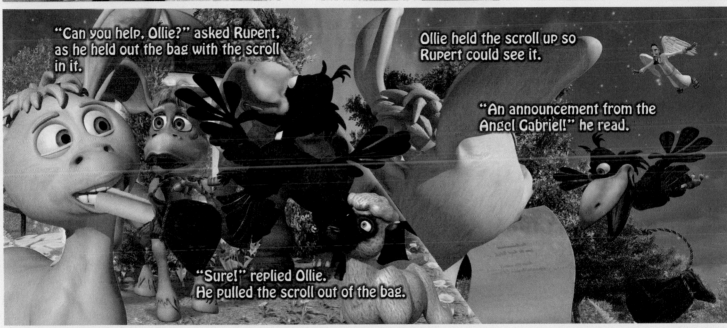

"Can you help, Ollie?" asked Rupert, as he held out the bag with the scroll in it.

Ollie held the scroll up so Rupert could see it.

"An announcement from the Angel Gabriel!" he read.

"Sure!" replied Ollie.
He pulled the scroll out of the bag.

At that moment, Angel Gabriel and picked up Rupert with the end of his finger!

Ollie rose off the ground, too! Both Ollie and Rupert were quite startled!

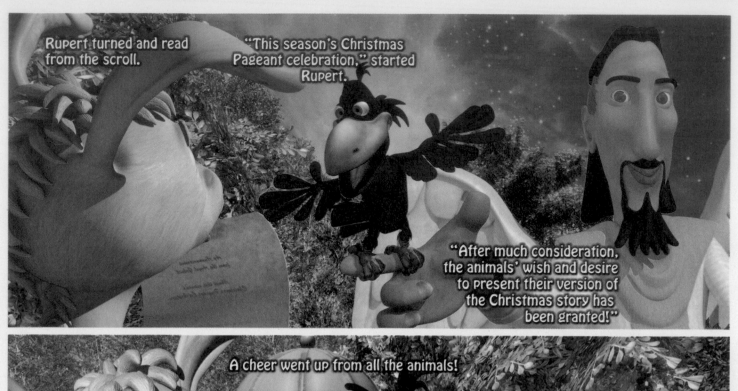

Rupert turned and read from the scroll.

"This season's Christmas Pageant celebration," started Rupert.

"After much consideration, the animals' wish and desire to present their version of the Christmas story has been granted!"

A cheer went up from all the animals!

Rupert continued.

"In the spirit of fairness, the animals will be allowed...'

"... to create their own sets." continued Rupert.

"And to invite all the children of Heaven to their own farm to view their pageant spectacle!"

The animals cheered again!

Gabriel gently set both Rupert and Ollie back down onto the ground. Ollie turned to Rupert.

"That's great news," said Ollie, "but how are we ever going to win if no one helps us?"

"Who is going to design our sets and make our costumes?"

"I don't know, Ollie," replied Rupert. "But I DO know we're in and there isn't much time!"

"Everyone!" yelled Rupert, turning to the gathered animals.

"I'll see you all at the old hay platform on the farm for our first production meeting in one hour!"

"And bring your talent with you!" he added.

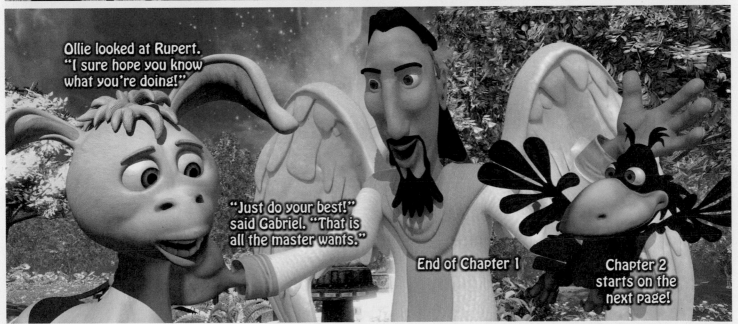

Ollie looked at Rupert. "I sure hope you know what you're doing!"

"Just do your best!" said Gabriel. "That is all the master wants."

End of Chapter 1

Chapter 2 starts on the next page!

Chapter 2:

The Auditions

An hour later, many animals gathered near the farm to hear what Rupert had to say. Even the dolphins were there!

"Hey, everyone!" Rupert yelled. "Settle down! I've got some really exciting news! This year, for the first time ever, the animals are going to WIN the Christmas pageant contest!"

"Wait a minute!" interrupted Aunt Alana. "How can you say we're going to win? The contest hasn't even started!"

"Yeah, Rupert!" added Ollie. "You don't want to give everyone false hopes!"

"I'm not lying!" protested Rupert. "I've been watching these Christmas pageants for years! Sure, all the contestants are great! I mean, how can you top a pageant when you have all the original characters in them?"

"Farmer John had quite an advantage," explained Rupert, "using the real Mary and the real Joseph and everybody else who was actually there!"

"But remember: this is a contest that will be judged by children! I know they will like us best!"

"We've GOT to win!" exclaimed Rupert.

"Well" said Ollie, "It's time to get down to brass tacks! Smoothfeather has written out some lines so we can hold auditions".

"We've got some important roles to fill!"

"So," continued Ollie, "reading for the part of the Three Wise Men from the East will be my brothers Esau, Isa and Jeremy!"

"I still don't know how these three ever got into Heaven!" complained Rupert.

"Rupert!" exclaimed Aunt Alana, "let them read their lines!"

Esau, Isa and Jeremy walked out onto the makeshift stage. Smoothfeather flew in front of them holding the script in his beak.

Isa began to read from the script.

"Golly! Look at that yonder star! It seems to be over Bethlehem!"

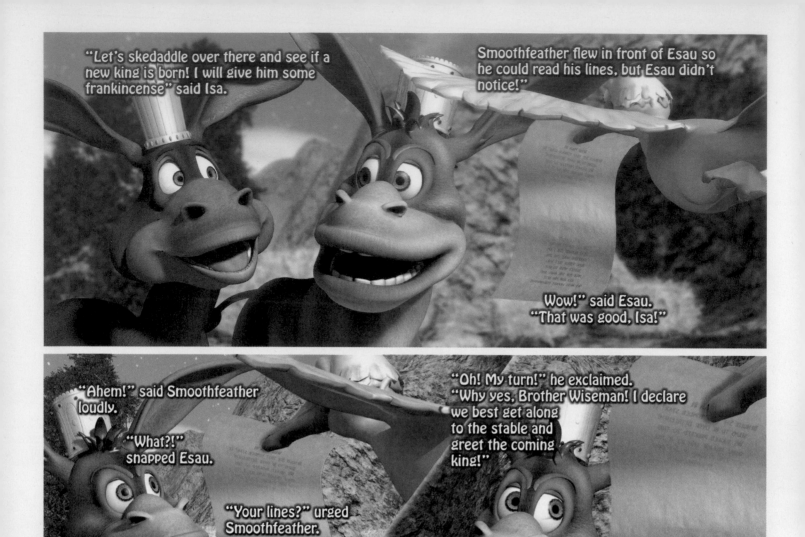

"Let's skedaddle over there and see if a new king is born! I will give him some frankincense" said Isa.

Smoothfeather flew in front of Esau so he could read his lines, but Esau didn't notice!"

Wow!" said Esau.
"That was good, Isa!"

"Ahem!" said Smoothfeather loudly.

"What?!" snapped Esau.

"Your lines?" urged Smoothfeather.

"Huh?" grunted Esau. Then he saw the script.

"Oh! My turn!" he exclaimed. "Why yes, Brother Wiseman! I declare we best get along to the stable and greet the coming king!"

"And I will bring him the gift of Myrrh!" added Esau.

"Don't forget ME, wise brothers!" added Jeremy, "for I am carrying gold for the king which they will surely need to buy milk for the baby and hay for his bed!"

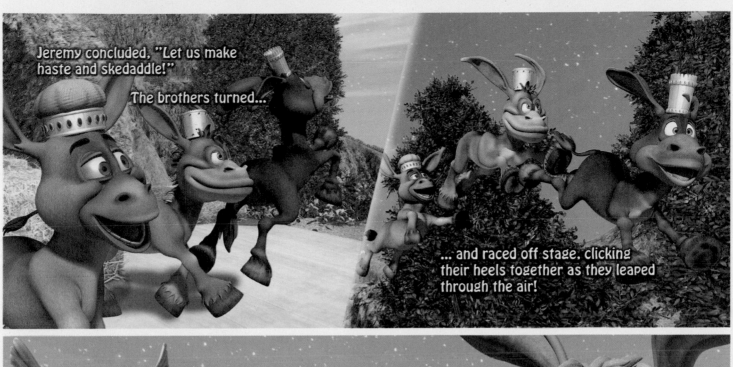

Jeremy concluded, "Let us make haste and skedaddle!"

The brothers turned...

... and raced off stage, clicking their heels together as they leaped through the air!

Everyone laughed and cheered! Ollie looked concerned.

"They were good, you have to admit," said Ollie cautiously, "but they aren't a shoe-in. This is a big role and there are others who want to be part of it!"

"So let me present to you... my friends, the elephants!" declared Ollie.

Hannibal, Massie and Muwanna all came up on stage, their front legs on each other's backs!

"... you're smarter than you look!"

"You there, in that pretty gown, looking so so sweet,"

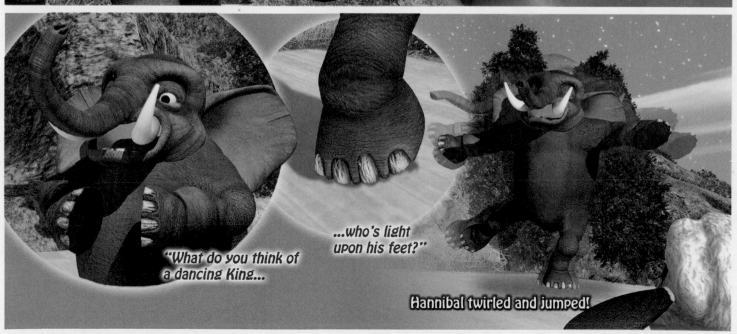

"What do you think of a dancing King...

...who's light upon his feet?"

Hannibal twirled and jumped!

Hannibal came down on the stage hard, nearly destroying it! Hay bales were thrown everywhere!

As everyone and everything settled, Muwanna dodged falling hay bales and made his way to the front of the stage.

He began to sing!

"You there, in that golden robe, with the flowers in your hair!"

"What do you think of a Persian King who can really...

SSSSSIIIIIII.......

...IIIIIIIINNNNNGGG!!!

Muwanna hit such a high note, everyone's ears hurt!

Massie walked to the edge of the stage and spoke to Whitey.

"You there, with your wool so light, were you really there that night?"

Massie looked off into the distance, and remembered.

"When we came to Bethlehem, and the stars came tumbling down!"

She put her trunk into a near-by water barrel...

... and sprayed the entire crowd!

The animals went crazy!

The three donkey brothers looked on, a bit disappointed.

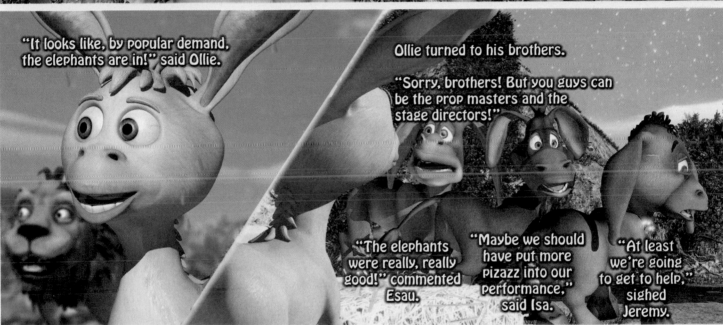

"It looks like, by popular demand, the elephants are in!" said Ollie.

Ollie turned to his brothers.

"Sorry, brothers! But you guys can be the prop masters and the stage directors!"

"The elephants were really, really good!" commented Esau.

"Maybe we should have put more pizazz into our performance," said Isa.

"At least we're going to get to help," sighed Jeremy.

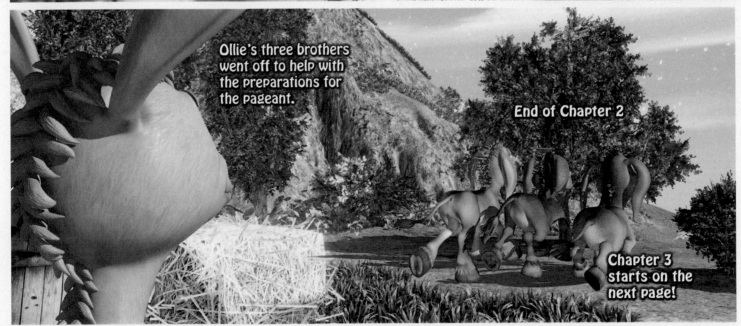

Ollie's three brothers went off to help with the preparations for the pageant.

End of Chapter 2

Chapter 3 starts on the next page!

Chapter 3:

Preparations

Rupert, Ollie and Thelonious began to plan for the pageant.

"Everyone!" exclaimed Rupert. "And I think we need to fix a fancy dinner for everyone at the pageant!"

"So how big of a crowd should we expect?" asked Thelonious.

"Dinner?" asked Hannibal. "But what will we make for them?"

"Look around you!" said Rupert, waving towards the fields of corn. "This farm grows everything! We can get Pontifer to help us with the menu. He can tell us what to make!"

"I like that idea!" said Ollie.

"We can have popcorn balls!" continued Ollie. "And pomegranate punch, egg nog, plum pudding, and sugar plums with sesame seeds!"

"I saw Jonathan and Rhea just a while ago. I'll ask them to help, too!"

"And let's make a great big gingerbread house, too!" added Ollie.

"Wait!" exclaimed Rupert. "Let's use the gingerbread house as the Nativity set! Then the kids can eat it when the show is over!"

"What a great idea!" said Hannibal.

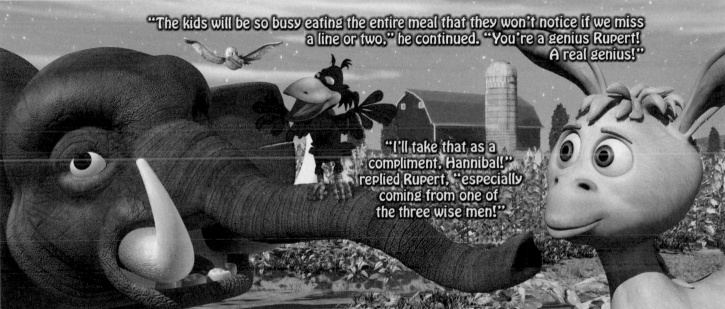

"The kids will be so busy eating the entire meal that they won't notice if we miss a line or two," he continued. "You're a genius Rupert! A real genius!"

"I'll take that as a compliment, Hannibal!" replied Rupert, "especially coming from one of the three wise men!"

There was suddenly a flurry of activity to be ready in time. Even humans helped! Pontifar, the kindly Egyptian cook, was helping to prepare the feast.

"We are going to need a lot more cream and eggs, Jonathan," said Pontifar. "Can you have a talk with the chickens and the cows?"

Emma led them both into the silo. Jonathan and Rhea looked around in amazement!

Huge golden eggs filled every shelf, all the way to the top of the silo!

"Egad!" exclaimed Jonathan. "Where did all those eggs come from?"

"The Lord has blessed us all with fruitfulness!" said Emma. "Now you can make the best gingerbread ever!"

Meanwhile, Donkey Ruthy was rehearsing one of the acts.

"Hark the Herald Angels sing, Glory to the newborn King!" sang the dolphins.

"All right!" said Ruthy. "That was very good! Now can you raise it up a few bars? And sing like you are really angels!"

"Sure!" answered Apollo. "Should we add some flying maneuvers?"

"That would be splendid! Work in some of those aerial maneuvers and we'll rehearse them tomorrow!"

Ruthy turned to leave.

"Now I've got to be going. The shepherds are having a very hard time and need lots of extra work!"

Ruthy headed off to the farm. She could not believe what she saw when she came through the corn!

Most of the animals were laboring hard. The creek was being re-routed, hay bales were being positioned as seats, and giant candy canes lined the aisles.

"This is beautiful!" exclaimed Ruthy.

As she walked down the aisle, Ruthy looked upon the three donkey brothers, licking the huge candy canes!

"What are you three up to now?" she asked.

"Nothing!" said Isa. He smiled and showed off his red teeth. "We're just trying to subdue the color a bit!"

"Yeah!" added Jeremy.

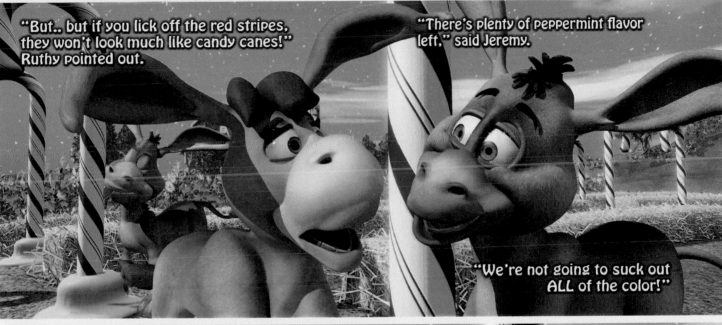

"But.. but if you lick off the red stripes, they won't look much like candy canes!" Ruthy pointed out.

"There's plenty of peppermint flavor left," said Jeremy.

"We're not going to suck out ALL of the color!"

"Yeah!" chimed in Esau. "Lighten up, Ruthy! Remember, this is a Christmas pageant, NOT Lent!"

"Oh, very well!" said Ruthy. "Hey, have you seen my sisters?

"I think they're down by the stage," Isa said, "helping with the costumes!"

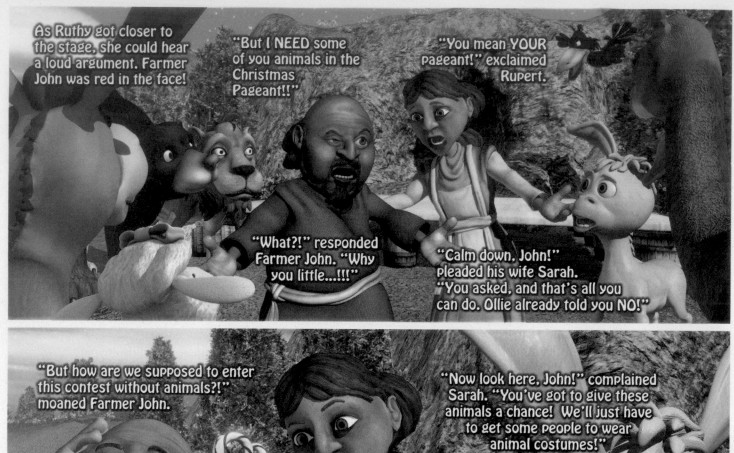

As Ruthy got closer to the stage, she could hear a loud argument. Farmer John was red in the face!

"But I NEED some of you animals in the Christmas Pageant!!"

"You mean YOUR pageant!" exclaimed Rupert.

"What?!" responded Farmer John. "Why you little...!!!"

"Calm down, John!" pleaded his wife Sarah. "You asked, and that's all you can do. Ollie already told you NO!"

"But how are we supposed to enter this contest without animals?!" moaned Farmer John.

"Now look here, John!" complained Sarah. "You've got to give these animals a chance! We'll just have to get some people to wear animal costumes!"

"How could you do this to me, Ollie? After all, you haven't a CHANCE of winning!!"

"Look, Farmer John," said Ollie, "I've got plenty to be grateful for. You've taken care of me for all of my life. But you have won this contest every year!"

"AND taken all the credit for it!" chimed in Rupert.

"What?!" cried Farmer John.

"That's right!" complained Rupert.

"While we animals slaved away in your pageants, YOU kept all the prizes! Your place is full of awards! If you are going to win again, you're just going to have to do it without the animals!"

"It's our turn now to show what we can do!'

Rupert began to sing:

"Without the animals beside you to decorate the set,

We will see pretty shortly, just who is the best!"

"This isn't personal or business!"    "It's the way it's got to be!"

"This Christmas, Farmer John, You won't have any donkeys! You won't have any sheep! You won't have any cows!"

Then Ollie began to sing:

"I can't be your donkey,
to carry you around.
Your wise men will be walking,
the camels are in our cast.
So sorry, Farmer John,
the time has come at last!"

Aunt Alana sang:
"I carried your Mary, your Baby,
your clothes!"

Then Muwanna sang:
"I carried the Wise Men.
I stubbed all my toes!"

One of the sheep sang:
"I baaahed 'til my throat
was so very sore!"

Everyone gathered around Farmer John
and joined in on the song!

"So sorry, Farmer John, we can't
help any more!"

"You're on your own this Christmas,
Just do the best you can!"

"You're on your own this Christmas,
Stand up and be a man!"

"This isn't fair!" cried Farmer John.
"It isn't fair at all!"

"But never mind! I have
almost all of the original
actors in our cast!"

"I'm STILL
going to win!"

Farmer John leaned in to Ollie and spoke in an angry, but sad voice.
"I never expected this from you, Ollie! From Rupert, yes!
But NOT from you!"

"Hey!" yelled
Rupert.

With that Farmer John stormed off in a huff, followed by his wife, who looked back apologetically.

Ollie turned to the group of animals.

"I'm really sorry he feels that way," he sighed.

"But remember," Ollie continued, "we can't let his sore feelings ruin the pageant. Everybody is excited to see our show, especially the children!"

"So let's go and put on the best pageant we can!"

"Hooray!" yelled all the animals.

With only two days before the pageant, everyone pitched in to help. The donkeys re-dug the creek so it was big enough for the dolphins and Jesus' throne.

The elephants helped fortify the stage and set up the curtain.

Even humans were helping! Jonathan and Rhea tried on the sheep costumes made from the wool sheared off of Whitey, Wooley and Snow.

Allondra, Jehu's wife, helped fit them with Shepherd's costumes. Thelonious the lion watched in awe.

"You little sheep look fabulous!" exclaimed Thelonious.

"They are doing very well!" said Allondra.

"Here, let me show you the costumes!"

"So, where is Jehu?" inquired Thelonious.

"He went to talk to some of the disciples about his father," said Allondra.

"Then you heard what happened this morning between Ollie and Farmer John?" Thelonious asked.

"Who hasn't?" replied Allondra.

"Farmer John thinks it's his right to win every year!" explained Allondra, as she helped adjust Wooley's shepherd costume.

"He has won so much, I think he believes it's his right to win! Why, even on Earth people learned to talked turns to help others!"

Then the sheep begin to sing.

"This will be the best
Christmas ever!

This will be the year
we get to rock!

We will be in this
all together,

Just on big bushy
happy flock!"

All three jumped up onto the stage!

"This is the beginning of
a new day,

The animals are rising
up to say!"

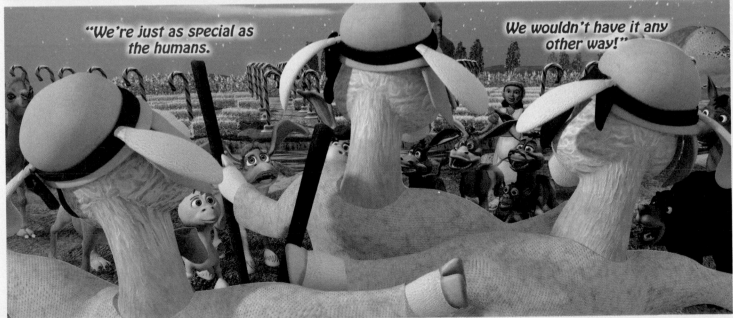

"We're just as special as
the humans.

We wouldn't have it any
other way!"

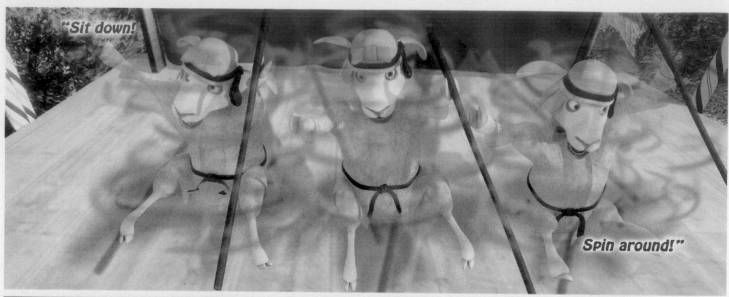

"It's the best Christmas show ever!"

A great cheer went up from the crowd that had gathered to listen.

"That's great, fellows!" encouraged Thelonious. "So we still need a Baby Jesus. Anybody got any ideas?"

Suddenly Wooley jumped off the stage and landed in front of Thelonious!

"Ooh! Ooh! I know who to get for Baby Jesus!" Wooley exclaimed.

"Who?" asked Thelonious.

Wooley was joined by Whitey and Snow.

"Who do YOU know?" asked Whitey.

"Yeah, who do YOU know?" questioned Snow.

Wooley turned to the other two.

"I was thinking... ...Tiny!" stated Wooley.

"Tiny?!" exclaimed Whitey. "Why he's perfect!"

"Yes, great idea!" added Snow.

"I know! He'll steal the show!" said Wooley.

Wooley turned to Thelonious. "You'll be going with an animal for Baby Jesus, right?" he asked.

"Uh, yeah! That's right," answered Thelonious.

"Well then, Tiny will be perfect... if you can talk him into auditioning!"

"Okay," said Thelonious. "But how do I find this Tiny?"

"Just ask Rupert!" called Wooley. "He knows how to find Tiny. Good Luck!"

End of Chapter 3

Turn the page to start Chapter 4!

Chapter 4:
About Farmer John

Meanwhile, in another part of Heaven, several of Jesus' disciples and friends gathered to discuss the situation involving Farmer John.

"I had a long talk with Jehu today," said Peter.

"This business with his father is getting troublesome!"

"Look," said Paul, "we all know Ollie's not the problem. He has never caused problems for anyone!"

"Well, at least anyone who was nice!" added Stephen.

"It's pretty natural," chimed in James, "for the kids to want to hang out with the animals. It is quite likely they are going to put on a spectacular show!"

"So what is Farmer John's problem?" asked Peter.

Paul thought for a moment.

"Do you think he might be spoiled from all his successes?" he asked.

"And maybe jealous?" added Stephan.

They all turned to Jesus for an answer.

Just then Jesus' pole began to shake. There was a fish on the line!

Jesus pulled in the fish.

"Catch and release. Catch and release," he sighed. "Just once I'd like to be able to fry up a few of these little fellows!"

The little fish desperately shook its head "NO!"

Jesus tossed the fish back. He took a deep breath.

"The purpose of this new Christmas pageant," said Jesus, "is to give the animals a chance to tell "The Story". Then all the children can see it from a different point of view."

"But Farmer John says that the animals are being unfair; that they are making it impossible for him to stage his regular show. He says that none of the animals will join his cast! He swears it's a boycott!"

"Can you blame them, Lord Jesus?" asked Stephen. "The animals just want a chance to be heard!"

"I know Farmer John pretty well," added Paul. "Why don't I go over and see if I can calm him down?"

Peter heard his stomach growl.

"All right," he said. "But since we're not eating these fish, did anyone bring any sandwiches?"

Jesus stood up. So did everyone else.

As Jesus began to sing, all five chairs sprang up into the air!

"I guess I'm expecting a miracle!"

The chairs twirled in the air, and turned into fruits and cakes!

"Farmer John has some growing to do!"

"Suppose the animals really win the hearts of the children?"

"Won't that be cute?"

They both walked across the water. Peter sang:

"See who the children love the most."

"That's who will win the Christmas feast!"

Peter and Jesus reached the bank.

Jesus began to sing again.

"Yes, it is Christmas in Heaven again, the children love this story so well."

Wherever Jesus walked, flowers grew!

"It's great to have new competition, let's ring out those Christmas bells!"

Jesus and his friends walked off as bells were heard coming from the distant Crystal City.

Meanwhile, Farmer John was continuing to add touches to his stable set.

With the stable sign in one hand and a hammer in the other, Farmer John reached up to nail in the sign at the peak of the stable.

The hammer came down hard...

YEOW!!!

... right on his thumb!

The sign popped off...

...and fell to the stage floor!

Farmer John's wife, Sarah, and his daughter Elizabeth were standing down below.

"Pomegranate juice, Daddy?" asked Elizabeth.

"Where's Jehu when I need him the most?!" yelled Farmer John as he came down the ladder.

"Is he helping the animals? My own son?! I can't build all these sets without him!"

He began to sing.

Elizabeth sang back.

"Daddy, Daddy Daddy don't
be foolish!
This is the greatest story
Heaven ever had!
You don't have to win
the pageant each and
every time!
Why can't we just give
them a hand?"

Then it was his wife's turn to sing!

"Now John, don't be so
pigheaded!

Things are different,
that's a fact!

But just do your best!
It's all you can do,

and trust that the
outcome is blessed!"

"Well," grumbled Farmer John,
"You can TALK about being
blessed, but I won't FEEL at
all blessed if I don't win!"

"Now John!" said Sarah, "Surely you
can find some charity in you heart for
the children!"

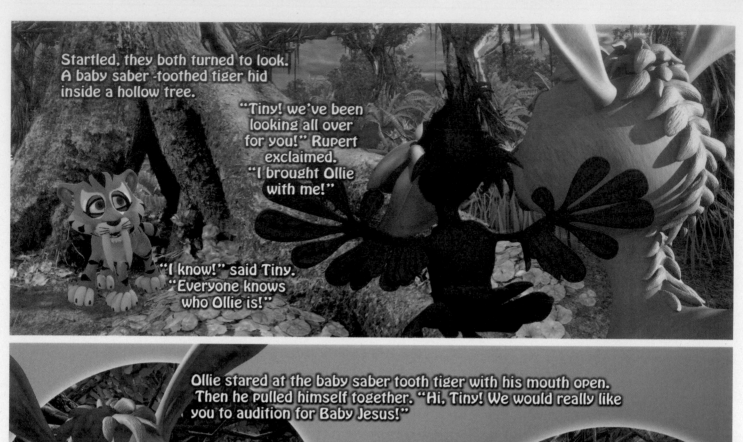

Startled, they both turned to look. A baby saber-toothed tiger hid inside a hollow tree.

"Tiny! we've been looking all over for you!" Rupert exclaimed. "I brought Ollie with me!"

"I know!" said Tiny. "Everyone knows who Ollie is!"

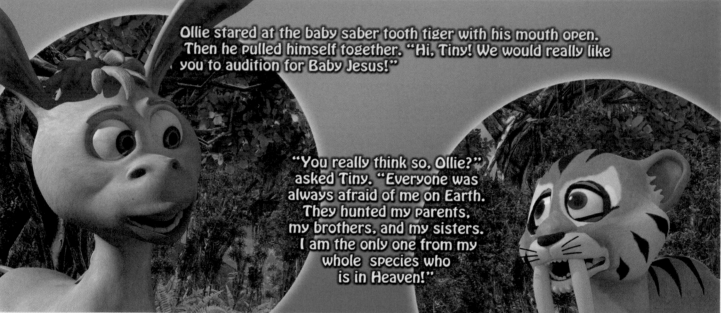

Ollie stared at the baby saber tooth tiger with his mouth open. Then he pulled himself together. "Hi, Tiny! We would really like you to audition for Baby Jesus!"

"You really think so, Ollie?" asked Tiny. "Everyone was always afraid of me on Earth. They hunted my parents, my brothers, and my sisters. I am the only one from my whole species who is in Heaven!"

"Look, Tiny." said Ollie. "I think you are perfect for the part! Sure, you're different, but look at me!

I'm different! When I was on Earth I was the only albino donkey in Israel! But God chose me for a special task!"

"Wow!" said Tiny.

"Maybe that is why we were directed to pick you for the role," continued Ollie. "You won't have any lines, and you sure won't scare any of the animals!

"Yeah!" added Rupert. "They'll think you're the cutest creature ever! When this is all over, you'll have so many visitors, they'll have to put a new road right to your tree!"

"Please say you will do it!" Ollie pleaded.

He began to sing.

"Please, please, please, Please say you'll do it!

Please say you'll give it you best!"

Say you'll do the part of Baby Jesus.

Please, please, please Just say "Yes!"

"Say you'll lay still in the manger, Say you'll smile and look so cute!

Tiny, we need you to make this Christmas pageant work!"

"No. I'm talkin' to the Boss... Mr. Rupert!" said the conductor.

"I'm just the casting director," replied Rupert. "Ollie's the REAL director!"

"Look, Rupert, we wouldn't be IN this show without your say so. Correct?"

"Oh hey," added Ollie, "you guys did a great job, We'll put it in the show! Right, Boss?"

"Right! Go with it!" said Rupert.

"How many more surprises do you have for me, Rupert?" teased Ollie.

"Thanks, Boss!" said the conductor. "Okay, everyone, take five!"

"Where I'm from, Ollie, pageants always had variety!"

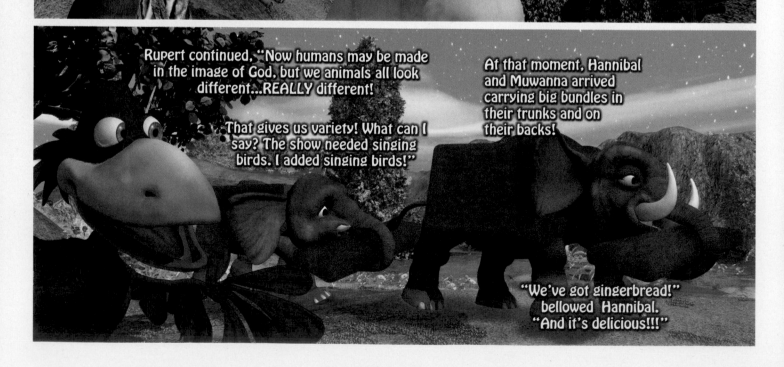

Rupert continued, "Now humans may be made in the image of God, but we animals all look different...REALLY different!

That gives us variety! What can I say? The show needed singing birds. I added singing birds!"

At that moment, Hannibal and Muwanna arrived carrying big bundles in their trunks and on their backs!

"We've got gingerbread!" bellowed Hannibal. "And it's delicious!!!"

Hannibal set down the gingerbread in his trunk.

"Emma gave us samples!" exclaimed Hannibal.

"I tell you, when we divide up this gingerbread nativity set at the end of the show and feed it to the audience, we can't help but get first place! It's terrific!!!"

Muwanna approached Ollie.

"Ollie, you need to get someone to watch Hannibal!" pleaded Muwanna.

"Why?" asked Ollie.

"He loves gingerbread too much! If someone doesn't watch him, he's liable to eat the whole set before the pageant!"

Hannibal began to sing.

"It's true! It's a fact! Don't have a heart attack!"

"This gingerbread's delicious! Every bite!"

"I'll wait 'till the 'wrap' to have another snack!"

"In the meantime, I'll practice all my lines!"

"Good!" said Ollie.
"Can both of you come over for the meeting after you've got the gingerbread arranged? We've got some exciting news!"

"We do?"
asked Rupert.

"Tiny?" Ollie
reminded him.

"Oh, yeah!"
remembered
Rupert.

"You two wouldn't want
to miss this meeting!"
finished Rupert.

"Can you see
anything?"
asked Abner.

"Yeah, they're definitely making progress,"
sighed Farmer John. "Looks like quite
a few humans are helping them out,
the traitors!"

"That's not good..."
said Abner.

"Wha... What?!"
stammered Farmer John.
"It's those kids of yours,
Abner! They're helping
Ollie! How COULD they?!"

"Kids!" moaned Abner.
"What can you do?"

"Oh, I'd like to tell THEM
a thing or two!" grumbled
Farmer John.

Suddenly, Paul's voice echoed
up into the tree. "What are
you two doing up there? Spying?"

"Whoa?!!" exclaimed a startled Abner.

He lost his grip on
the tree and started
to fall!

... taking Farmer John with him!

Farmer John sat up. His spy glass was broken into several pieces!

"Tarnation, Farmer John!" exclaimed Paul. "You shouldn't be spying on the animals! Why is winning so important to you?!"

"There's other ways to win besides spying," said Paul.

"There's only one way to win... the old fashioned way," added Abner. "You do whatever it takes, even if it means stepping on some toes!"

"That's what my pop-in-law has been telling me!"

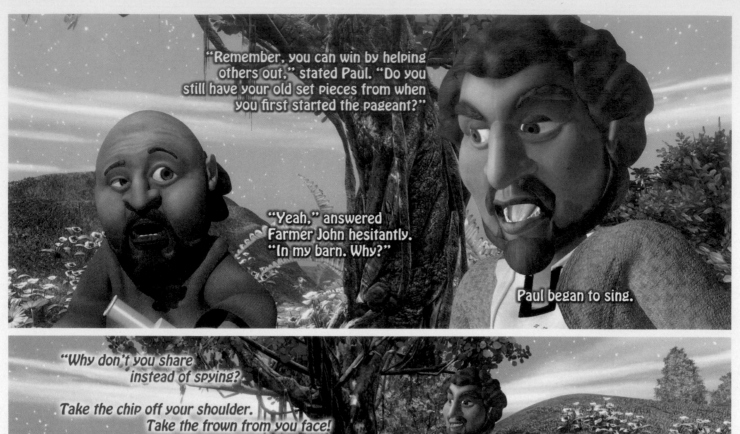

"Remember, you can win by helping others out," stated Paul. "Do you still have your old set pieces from when you first started the pageant?"

"Yeah," answered Farmer John hesitantly. "In my barn. Why?"

Paul began to sing.

"Why don't you share instead of spying?

Take the chip off your shoulder. Take the frown from you face!

Take the time just to reach out,

Put yourself in their place."

"They're struggling for your acceptance.

They're trying hard just to please!"

"Why don't you give them a hand up?"

"Take a moment, do a good deed!"

"A good deed, it will cheer you up immensely, a good deed, will change your point of view."

"A good deed will warm your heart intensely.

A good deed is just what they deserve."

Abner stood up, brushing off the dust.

"That's more than just a good idea, Farmer John. You've got to admit you've been pretty miserable lately!"

Farmer John sighed. "I guess you're right, Paul. I've been so focused on winning that I totally forgot the Golden Rule..."

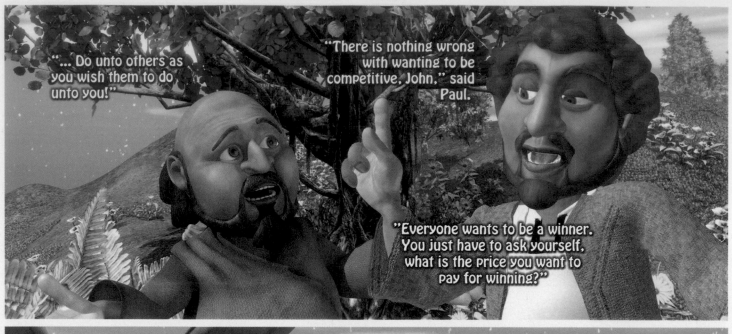

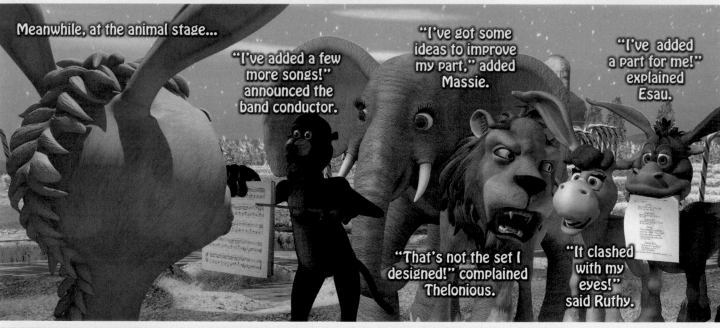

Ollie took a deep breath. "Now I have some GOOD news!" he said. "After much consideration, we have picked our Baby Jesus..."

"...Tiny!"

The bundle in Muwanna's trunk began to move!

Suddenly, Tiny popped up!

He tumbled out, hung by one tooth for a moment,

... then dropped to the stage floor.

The crowd went wild! All the animals cheered!

"Tiny, I think the children are going to love you as Baby Jesus!" exclaimed Thelonious enthusiastically.

"Wow! Thank you!" was all Tiny could think of to say.

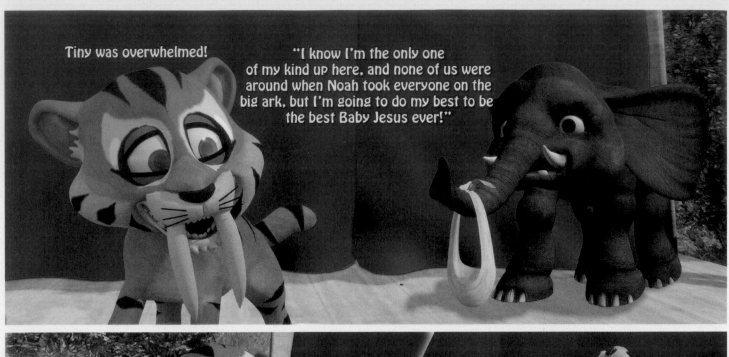

Tiny was overwhelmed!

"I know I'm the only one of my kind up here, and none of us were around when Noah took everyone on the big ark, but I'm going to do my best to be the best Baby Jesus ever!"

Tiny began to sing!

"I'll be the best Baby Jesus ever! I'll cuddle and I'll coo!"

"I'll be the best Baby Jesus! Everyone will think I'm cute!"

"I know I've got two big teeth. and stripes from ear-to-ear!

But when I'm in the manger, you'll think that I'm so dear!"

"I'll be the best Baby Jesus, Best Baby Jesus!

Better than all the rest!

I'll be the best Baby Jesus ever, One you won't forget!"

As Tiny continued to sing, Thelonious turned to Ollie.

"Well," commented Thelonious, "one thing is for sure... Tiny isn't troubled by thoughts of inadequacy or inferiority. It looks like he's going to play his part with confidence!"

Just then, Farmer John and Abner were hauling a cart of stage sets and props over the hill to the animal stage.

"Listen!" said Farmer John. "Do I hear singing? RATS!!"

"Father!" panted Abner. "I think... I need... to stop... and rest!"

"Nonsense, Abner! It's just over the hill!" said Farmer John. "I let you talk me into this, but the sooner we get it over with, the better!"

They got the cart to the top of the hill. Abner stopped to rest, but the cart kept going!

"Nice!" said Farmer John.

"That's a much better speed, Abner!"

The cart picked up speed as it went downhill, taking Farmer John with it!

"Hey!" complained Farmer John. "That's a bit too fast, Abner... Abner?"

"ABNER!!!"

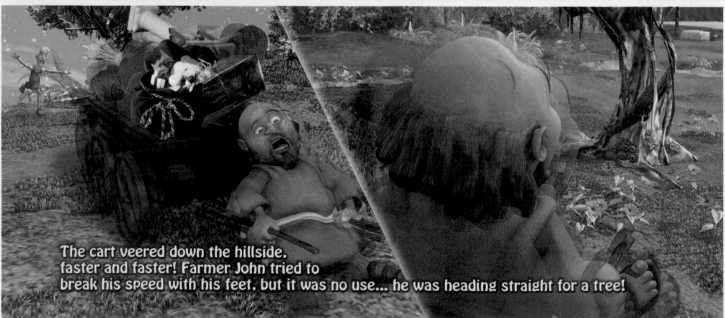

The cart veered down the hillside, faster and faster! Farmer John tried to break his speed with his feet, but it was no use... he was heading straight for a tree!

Suddenly the big tree shook, startling all the tropical birds!

"Ow! Ow! Ow!!" complained Farmer John from below.

The animals rushed over.

"Farmer John! Are you all right?" asked Ollie.

"Just... peachy!" Farmer John moaned, rubbing his bottom.

Rupert flew over and looked in the cart. "Wow!" he said. "These set pieces look terrific!"

"Well, it wasn't my idea to share," replied Farmer John as he struggled to get up. "But you all enjoy them!"

"Hannibal," asked Rupert, "will you take Farmer John over to the stream to wash up?"

"Sure!" answered Hannibal.

"Hey!" yelled Farmer John. "Wait!"

Hannibal set Farmer John down into the creek.

"You rest here a bit, little fellow," said the big elephant. "We'll unload the set pieces. And thanks for being square with us!"

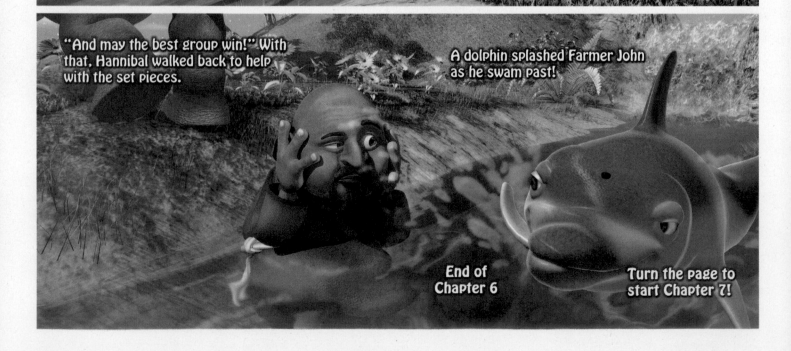

"And may the best group win!" With that, Hannibal walked back to help with the set pieces.

A dolphin splashed Farmer John as he swam past!

End of Chapter 6

Turn the page to start Chapter 7!

Chapter 7:
The Secret Valley

A little while later, both Farmer John and Abner were back at work on their pageant sets.

The cut-out animals looked nice, but it was obvious they were not real.

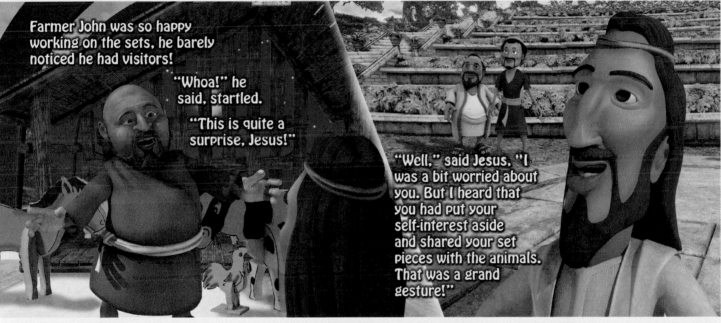

Farmer John was so happy working on the sets, he barely noticed he had visitors!

"Whoa!" he said, startled.

"This is quite a surprise, Jesus!"

"Well," said Jesus, "I was a bit worried about you. But I heard that you had put your self-interest aside and shared your set pieces with the animals. That was a grand gesture!"

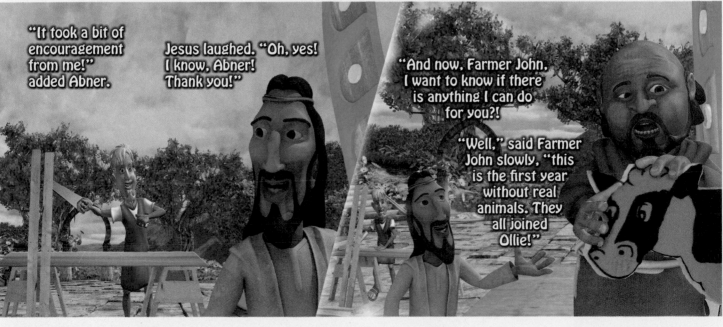

"It took a bit of encouragement from me!" added Abner.

Jesus laughed. "Oh, yes! I know, Abner! Thank you!"

"And now, Farmer John, I want to know if there is anything I can do for you?!

"Well," said Farmer John slowly, "this is the first year without real animals. They all joined Ollie!"

"I think we can help you there, John!" said Peter.

"I think so, too!" added James.

Farmer John looked puzzled as he followed Peter and James.

Farmer John looked on, amazed, as James and Peter ushered him onto a floating cloud!

"Oh my!" was all he could say as the cloud lifted off.

The cloud traveled quickly over the beautiful country side.

"So THIS is how you two get around so fast!" exclaimed Farmer John.

"Yes," said Peter. "It's one of the perks of management!"

The cloud landed among animals of all kinds. Farmer John stepped out.

"This is... amazing!!!" was all he could say.

"Here are all animals you need!" said Peter.

"And they'll be more than happy to go with you!" James added.

"I was foolish to think that if I gave to others," Farmer John explained, "I wouldn't have everything I needed. I was missing the whole spirit of Christmas...

...That God loved the world and gave his only begotten son, so whoever believed would have Heaven eternally..."

"... and not miss all of THIS!" Farmer John exclaimed.

"It's a long journey back," said James. "Just follow the stream and it will lead right back to the Crystal City!"

"And don't worry about the animals," Peter added.

"They will have plenty of grazing land and water during the journey!"

The cloud rose from the ground.

And remember," added Peter, "you can never out-give God!" With that, they flew away.

"Good-bye!" yelled Farmer John. "And thank you!"

"So," said Farmer John, turning back toward all the animals,

"So which ones do I chose? And how do I get them all back? I could sure use the help!"

Just then, he heard laughing and splashing coming from a nearby stream.

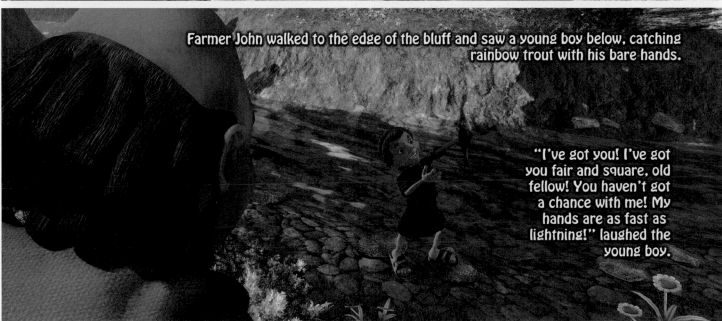

Farmer John walked to the edge of the bluff and saw a young boy below, catching rainbow trout with his bare hands.

"I've got you! I've got you fair and square, old fellow! You haven't got a chance with me! My hands are as fast as lightning!" laughed the young boy.

"You down there!" yelled Farmer John. "I could use some help!"

"What kind of help?" asked the boy.

"Sure! I'll be right there!" replied the boy.

He tossed the fish back. "Good-bye, old fellow!"

"I'm taking some of these animals back to the Crystal City. I need them for the Christmas pageant. Can you help me?"

The boy climbed up the embankment. Farmer John put out his hand.

"Hi, there! Thanks for the help. I'm Farmer John. What's your name?"

"I'm Meddi. You're not THE Farmer John from Bethany, are you?"

"The one and the same!" replied Farmer John.

"At last we meet!" said Meddi. "I know Ollie and Elizabeth!"

Meddi and Farmer John looked on as a memory bubble formed behind them...

"Way back then, I ran with a pretty bad crowd... Bandits!"

"We stole your donkeys," Meddi continued, "and tied up your two children in a net! They were hanging from a tree, directly above a pack of hungry jackals!"

"Ollie told me stealing was bad, and I listened. I guess that's why I'm here in Heaven, instead of... well, you know where!"

"After Ollie got away to rescue Jehu and Elizabeth, I helped deliver his brothers to the wine merchant, Gallius!"

"I saw my chance to escape and I sneaked onto the ship. But it sank in a big storm, and I perished with it!"

The memory bubble popped!

"As I was drowning, an angel came and rescued me. That's why I'm here. I... I'm awfully sorry about what I did!"

"That was a long time ago, Meddi," replied Farmer John softly.

"Don't worry about it. None of us lived a perfect life on Earth. Jesus forgave you... and I forgive you, too!"

"Now let's get these animals to the pageant! We only have a day left! Are you up for it?"

"Who do you think I am?" protested Farmer John. "Some old man? Lead on!!"

"Up for it? I sure am!" replied Meddi with enthusiasm. "A new adventure is just what I need! And I can show you a shortcut, but it does take us over some steep ground!"

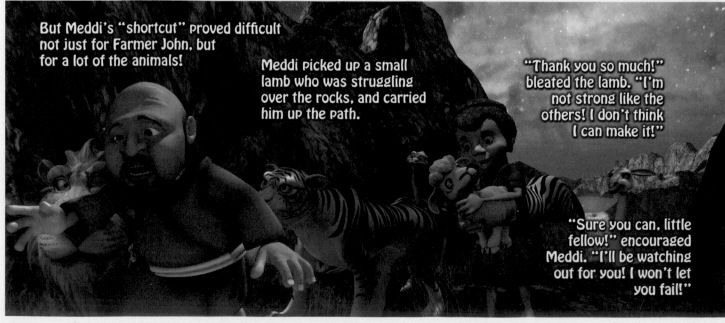

But Meddi's "shortcut" proved difficult not just for Farmer John, but for a lot of the animals!

Meddi picked up a small lamb who was struggling over the rocks, and carried him up the path.

"Thank you so much!" bleated the lamb. "I'm not strong like the others! I don't think I can make it!"

"Sure you can, little fellow!" encouraged Meddi. "I'll be watching out for you! I won't let you fail!"

Meddi began to sing as he turned to the other animals.

"Come on! Come on! Don't lag behind!

Come on, come on, You'll be just fine!"

"Let's go, let's go let's climb the hill!

Come little lamb, Don't stand there so still!"

"Off we go, away, away!

Another wonderful Heaven Day!"

"The weather's great, the air's so clear,

It's heavenly! Everything's shining from here!"

End of Chapter 7

Turn the page to start Chapter 8!

**Chapter 8:**

**The Build-up!**

Rehearsals continued for Ollie's pageant, scheduled to open that night. Ollie and Ruthy watched as the dolphins went through their act.

Meanwhile, Rupert flew up to Malachi the Angel, a roll of posters held tightly in his claws.

"Say, Malachi! Do you suppose you can help me out a bit?" asked Rupert.

"Sure, brother Rupert!" answered Malachi. "How can I help you?"

"I'm trying to get all these posters for the pageant out today," said Rupert. "My wings are tired, and I've got a long way to go!"

"Sure!" exclaimed Malachi. "I'd love to help! Hop on!"

With Malachi's help, Rupert's posters started to appear all over the Crystal City.

And they told people by word-of-mouth.

"Hey, don't forget to bring the kids to "Christmas in Heaven", the best Christmas pageant ever! WITH the original stars from the era!" yelled Rupert.

"Wouldn't dream of missing it!" came the reply.

With a big thanks, Rupert jumped off Malachi's back and flew down, clutching the last poster. A group of children gathered below.

"Hey, kids!" he yelled, "Are you coming to the best show ever?"

"What show?" one of them asked.

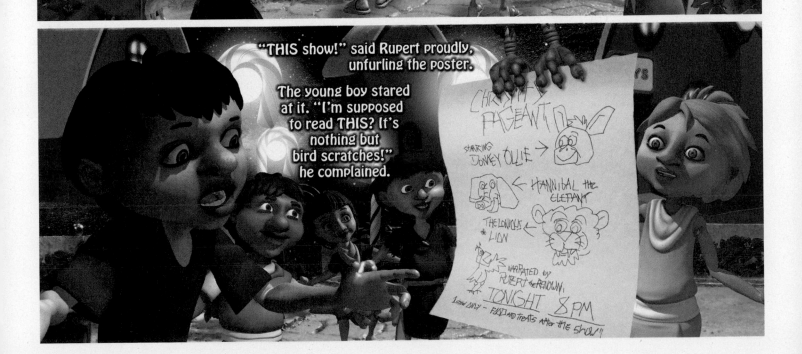

"THIS show!" said Rupert proudly, unfurling the poster.

The young boy stared at it. "I'm supposed to read THIS? It's nothing but bird scratches!" he complained.

CHRISTMAS PAGEANT

STARRING DONKEY OLLIE →

← HANNIBAL THE ELEFANT

THE LONIOUS THE LION ←

NARRATED by RUPERT the RENOWN,

TONIGHT 8 PM

1 SHOW ONLY - FOOD AND TREATS AFTER THE SHOW!!

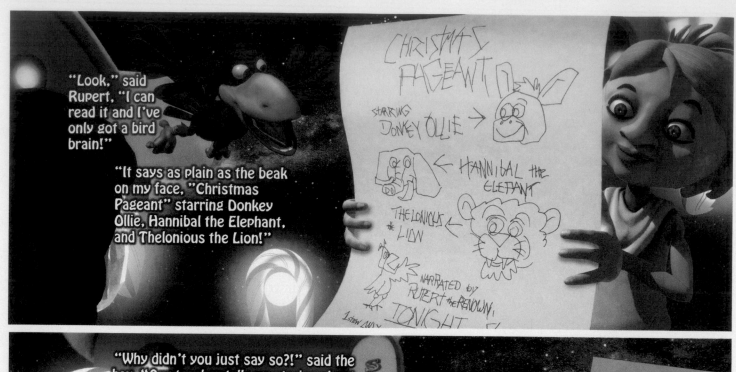

"Look," said Rupert, "I can read it and I've only got a bird brain!"

"It says as plain as the beak on my face, "Christmas Pageant" starring Donkey Ollie, Hannibal the Elephant, and Thelonious the Lion!"

"Why didn't you just say so?!" said the boy. "Our teacher tells us stories about Donkey Ollie, Hannibal and Thelonious all the time!"

"Did she ever tell you stories about Rupert the Renown?" asked Rupert, somewhat concerned.

"RUMOR the renown?" asked the boy.

"NO, NO, NO! Not Rumor... RUPERT, silly!" he corrected. "I'm going to be the narrator. If it wasn't for me saving their hides, I doubt if any of them would have made it into Heaven!"

Rupert began to sing.

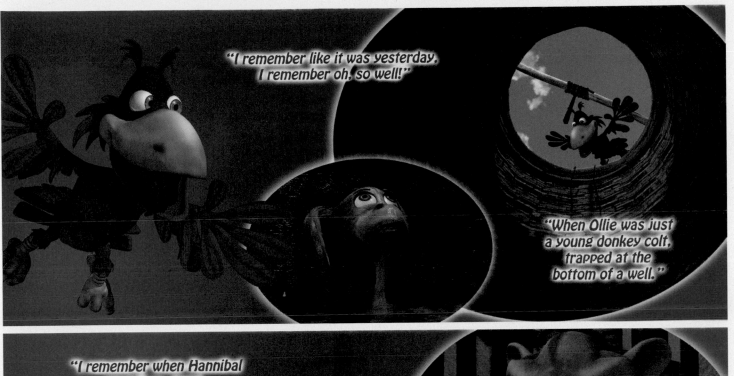

"I remember like it was yesterday, I remember oh, so well!"

"When Ollie was just a young donkey colt, trapped at the bottom of a well."

"I remember when Hannibal wasn't so great, He was chained to a pole!"

"And the Lion King was starving for days, and treated like a fool!"

"I was there to make it happen, facilitate escapes.

I delivered many messages, helped many avoid bad fate!"

"I was the unsung
hero of yesteryear!

It's true, it really is!

If Rupert the Renown
had not been around,

things wouldn't be like they is!"

"That's amazing!" exclaimed
a young boy.

"Just one of my
many tricks!"
said Rupert,
dizzily.

"Do it again!"
asked a small
girl.

"No, I don't
think so!"
replied Rupert.

"But come see the
pageant. You'll
really get a kick
out of it!"

Rupert began singing again.

"If you miss this play,
you are foolish!

You won't get
a second chance.

To watch the true blue characters,
act and sing and dance!"

"So take the flyer,
tell a friend.

We don't like singing
to an empty house!"

"Make sure to sit close to the stage,
and be quiet as a mouse!"

With that, Rupert
flew off to get ready
for the pageant!

Meanwhile, Farmer John was
struggling to get the animals
through a high mountain pass.
He was exhausted!

"That... did it!" wheezed
Farmer John. "I can't go...
a single step further! This
is absolutely useless! I'll
NEVER get the animals to
my pageant in time!"

"Is that such a bad thing?"
echoed a distant voice.

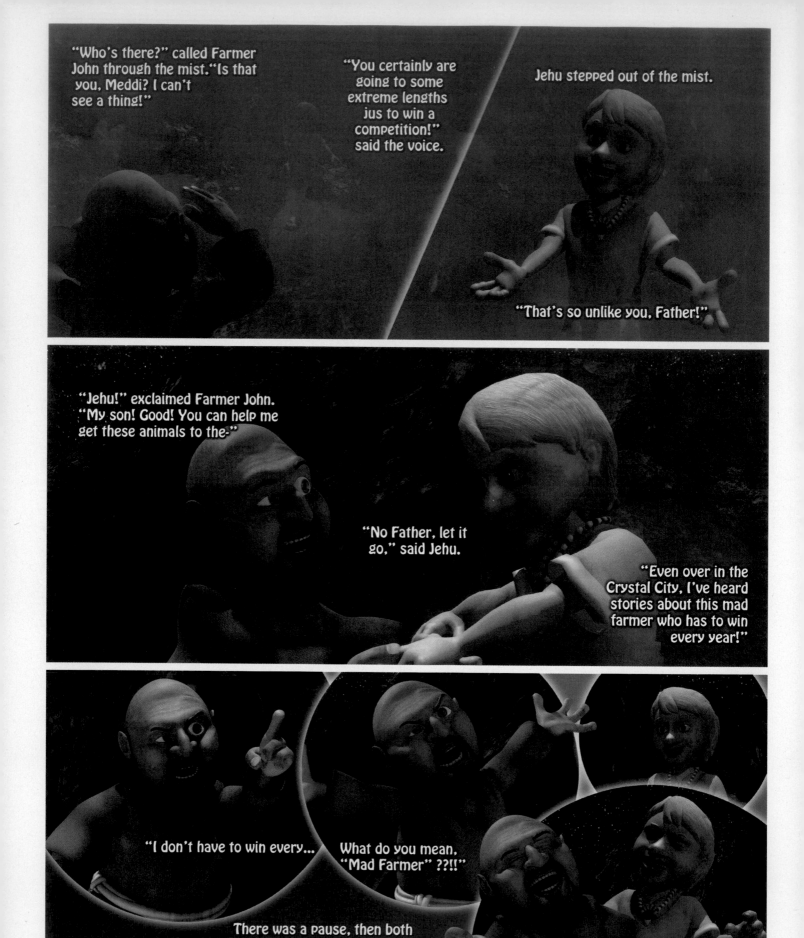

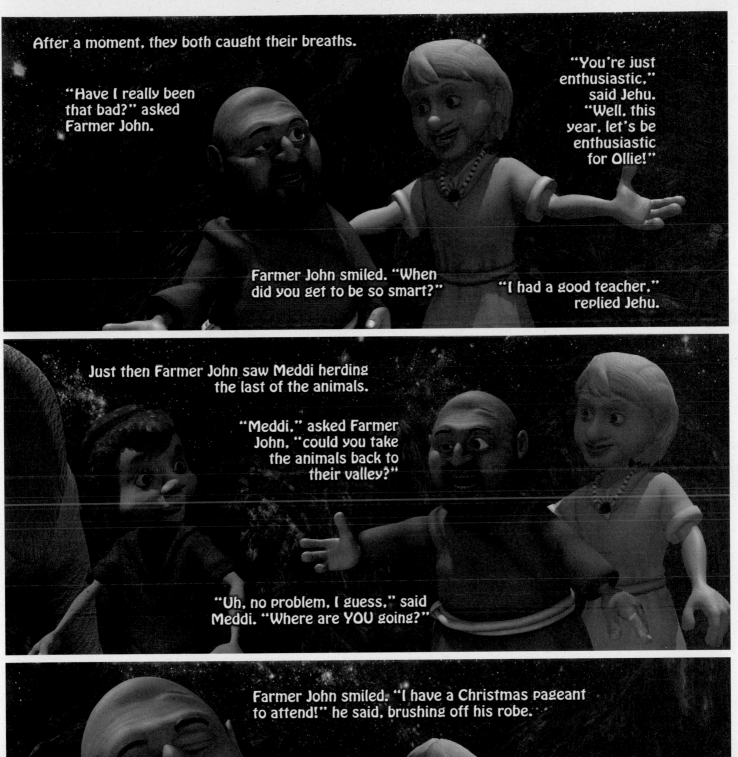

After a moment, they both caught their breaths.

"Have I really been that bad?" asked Farmer John.

"You're just enthusiastic," said Jehu. "Well, this year, let's be enthusiastic for Ollie!"

Farmer John smiled. "When did you get to be so smart?"

"I had a good teacher," replied Jehu.

Just then Farmer John saw Meddi herding the last of the animals.

"Meddi," asked Farmer John, "could you take the animals back to their valley?"

"Uh, no problem, I guess," said Meddi. "Where are YOU going?"

Farmer John smiled. "I have a Christmas pageant to attend!" he said, brushing off his robe.

End of Chapter 8

Turn the page for the last chapter!

Chapter 9:

The Pageant

As early evening approached, the amphitheater began to fill with people of all ages.

Ollie peeked through the curtain to see the throne in the middle of the pond. Thelonious joined him.

"They brought HIS throne about an hour ago," said Thelonious. He turned to Ollie. "Nervous?" he asked.

"A little, yeah," admitted Ollie.

"Look!" added Ollie, "the children are already arriving! I... I never knew there were so many children in Heaven!"

"I suppose that's what makes it Heaven, Ollie!" answered Thelonious. "For what is more pure than the heart of an innocent child?"

"Wow!" exclaimed Rupert. "Thousands of children are on the way! I hope we have enough pomegranate juice!"

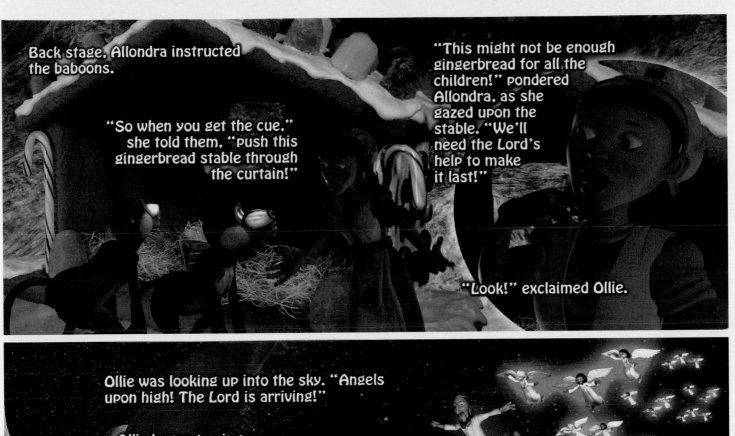

Back stage, Allondra instructed the baboons.

"So when you get the cue." she told them, "push this gingerbread stable through the curtain!"

"This might not be enough gingerbread for all the children!" pondered Allondra, as she gazed upon the stable. "We'll need the Lord's help to make it last!"

"Look!" exclaimed Ollie.

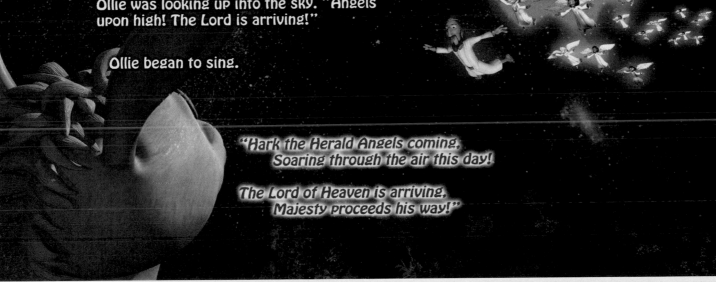

Ollie was looking up into the sky. "Angels upon high! The Lord is arriving!"

Ollie began to sing.

"Hark the Herald Angels coming,
    Soaring through the air this day!

The Lord of Heaven is arriving,
    Majesty proceeds his way!"

"The hosts of Heaven are rejoicing,
    The children are in rapturous awe!

He alone creation's ruler,
    Jesus Christ, the Lord of all!"

"We're rocking today!
Gathered for the Christmas play,

It's Christmas in Heaven,
The greatest place in the world!"

"It's Christmas, it's Christmas, just like years ago!"

"The shepherds were gathered, tending to their flocks!"

The children went crazy! The flying dolphins, the jumping children dressed as sheep, and the real sheep pretending to be shepherds were almost too much for them!

Rupert appeared from the back of the amphitheater and flew toward the stage.

"It was a busy season in Bethlehem!" said Rupert.

"Joseph could find no room for Mary," continued Rupert, "who was about to give birth to Jesus!"

Ollie turned to the baboons. "Here he comes!" he whispered loudly. "Push the set on!!!"

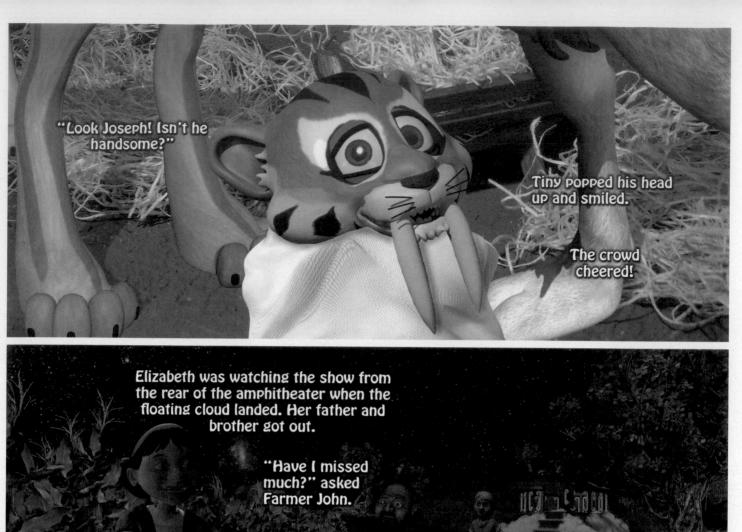

"Look Joseph! Isn't he handsome?"

Tiny popped his head up and smiled.

The crowd cheered!

Elizabeth was watching the show from the rear of the amphitheater when the floating cloud landed. Her father and brother got out.

"Have I missed much?" asked Farmer John.

"Oh, Father!" cried Elizabeth, giving him a big hug, "I'm SO glad you made it!"

"No, you haven't missed much!"

"Good!" replied Farmer John.

Suddenly the audience broke out in more cheers. They all looked toward the stage.

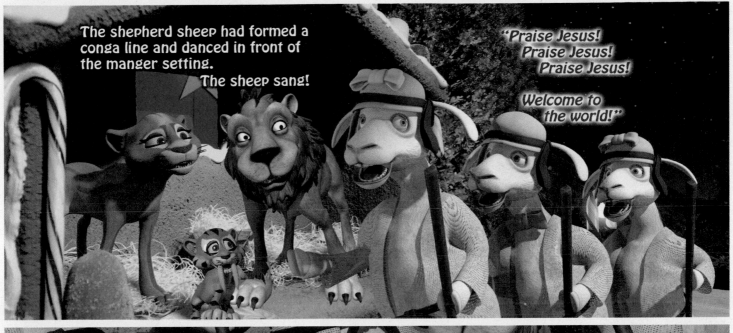

The shepherd sheep had formed a conga line and danced in front of the manger setting.

The sheep sang!

"Praise Jesus! Praise Jesus! Praise Jesus!

Welcome to the world!"

Tiny stepped out onto the stage. He looked around, star-struck!

"Praise Jesus! Praise Jesus! Praise Jesus!

You're such a cute boy!"

Thelonious looked off-stage to see Ollie trying to get Tiny's attention.

"Praise Jesus! Praise Jesus! Praise Jesus!

Emmanuel our God!"

"Tiny!" whispered Ollie, "Tiny! Get back in the manger!"

Thelonious stepped forward and picked up Tiny...

...just as the shepherd sheep finished their song!

"Praise Jesus! Praise Jesus! Praise Jesus!

"You bring the world such joy!"

Rupert continued his speech from the top of the stable.

"Three Wise Men and their caravan traveled for days!"

The spotlight swung to the back of the amphitheater and onto the three elephants.

"They brought gifts of frankincense, myrrh and gold to the newborn king!"

Hannibal pulled a large golden circus wagon. On top, baboons were throwing out golden beads to the children below!

Muwanna pulled a giant urn filled with aromatic spices...

...followed by Massie, who hauled a cart with bolts of fabric, a crown of burning incense on her head.

"The three wise men sought information from King Herod, who told them the scriptures indicated a Messiah would be born in Bethlehem!" Rupert announced.

"The star of David guided them to the manger!" concluded Rupert.

The elephants began to sing!

"Gold, gold, gold for the King,
This precious, precious gold,
Lord do we bring!"

"We the wise Magi,

Here to see the King,
Gold, gold, gold do we bring!"

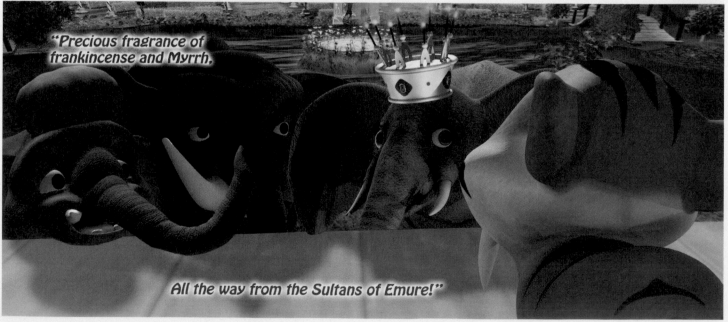

"Precious fragrance of frankincense and Myrrh,

All the way from the Sultans of Emure!"

"A fitting gift for a child the immortal Lord of Lords,

these precious gifts do we bring!"

"Everyone's padding their part!" sighed Ollie.

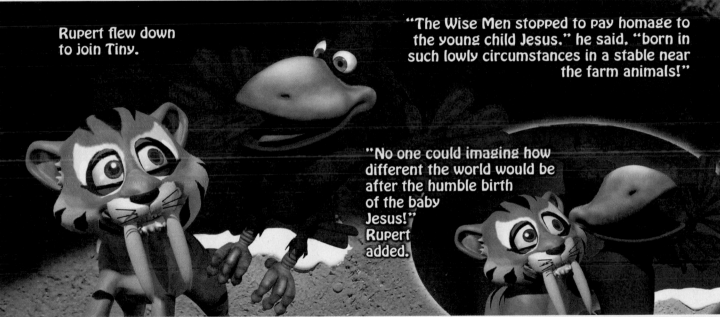

Rupert flew down to join Tiny.

"The Wise Men stopped to pay homage to the young child Jesus." he said. "born in such lowly circumstances in a stable near the farm animals!"

"No one could imaging how different the world would be after the humble birth of the baby Jesus!" Rupert added.

Rupert continued.

"The Wise Men spoke of a warning from an angel. He told them not to return to King Herod, or to tell him where the baby Jesus was. They knew Herod would try to harm the child!"

Thelonious spoke as Joseph. "Thank you so much, Magi, for the treasures you have showered upon us. We will take these gifts and flee into Egypt. Herod won't follow us there!"

The lioness who played Mary spoke. "My heart is overjoyed with the many visitors that have welcomed my son!"

"May God be with you on your journey back to your land." she said.

"We are sad you are leaving, Mary and Joseph, for surely your son has brought light to our hearts and to the world!" said Whitey the sheep.

"We would like to accompany you to Egypt and protect you while you are there!" added Wooley.

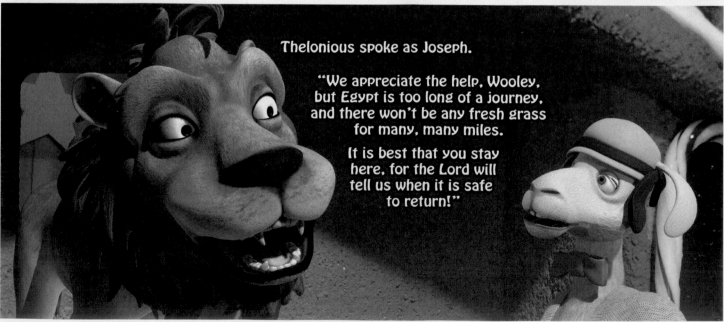

Thelonious spoke as Joseph.

"We appreciate the help, Wooley, but Egypt is too long of a journey, and there won't be any fresh grass for many, many miles.

It is best that you stay here, for the Lord will tell us when it is safe to return!"

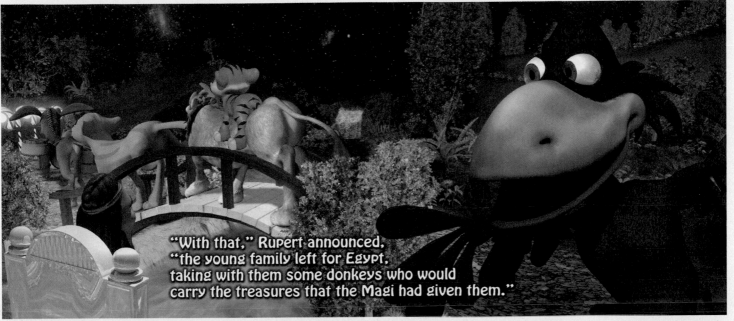

"With that," Rupert announced, "the young family left for Egypt, taking with them some donkeys who would carry the treasures that the Magi had given them."

The audience erupted in applause, clapping and shouting "Hallelujah" and "Glory to the Lord!"

The dolphins began their water show in front of King Jesus.

They raced through the water and gracefully sailed over the throne!

Jesus was delighted!

A tear of pride ran down Farmer John's face.

The cast gathered in front of the pond for a curtain call, singing!

"We worship you,
King Jesus,
sitting on your throne!"

"You reign on high
the heavens cry
your praise
for evermore!"

"We worship you,
King Jesus!
the glory's
all your own!"

Children began to swarm toward the stage. Jehu and Farmer John walked up to Ollie and Rupert.

"Great show, everyone!" said Jehu.

"That was a terrific production, Ollie!" added Farmer John.

"Thanks, Farmer John!" replied Ollie.

"We're sorry you didn't get your production going," Rupert said. "But maybe next year we can all work together!"

"My, my, my!" exclaimed Hannibal, as he tore off a piece of the set. "This gingerbread is delicious!"

"What about it, Farmer John? Next year we all do the pageant together. But the animals get to speak and sing as well. Is it a deal?"

Farmer John was silent for a moment. Then he spoke.

"Sure!" he replied. "After all, how can you have Christmas spirit without giving and doing good for others? Yes, it's a deal!"

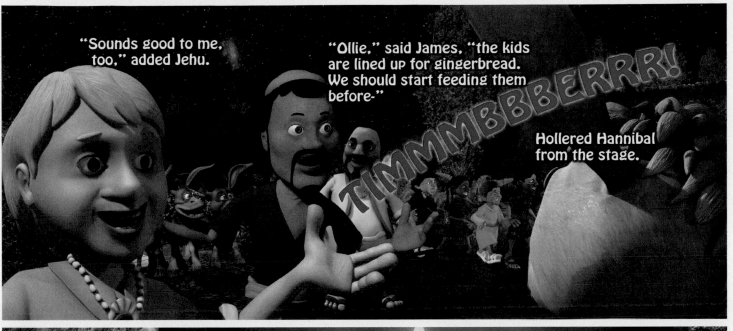

"Sounds good to me, too," added Jehu.

"Ollie," said James, "the kids are lined up for gingerbread. We should start feeding them before-"

TIMMMBBBERRR!

Hollered Hannibal from the stage.

CRASH!!

With that, the gingerbread set came tumbling down. Candy popped off and flew everywhere!

All the children swarmed over the broken set, tearing off chunks of the delicious gingerbread.

"Hey, Ollie! First come, first serve!" Muwanna yelled.

Ollie smiled.

Up on stage, Ollie's brothers were also discovering the joys of gingerbread!

"This stuff is much better than hay!" said Jeremy.

"This stuff is much better than oats!" said Isa.

"This stuff is even better than fresh carrots!" Esau proclaimed. "I can't wait for Christmas again!"

Esau began to sing.

"I can't wait for Christmas
to come rolling along!"

Jeremy sang.

"I love the three
Wise Men the best!"

Then it was Muwanna's turn.

"I love the angels
singing in the hills!"

"I love the Star of Bethlehem, shining oh, so bright!"

sang Tiny.

"The escape to Egypt is a thrill!"

added Thelonious.

The entire group sang.

"We can't wait for Christmas again!"

"Visiting with family and friends!"

Farmer John chimed in.

"I can't wait for Christmas to sing some happy songs!"

Everyone sang,

"I can't wait for Christmas to come rolling along!"